For Beth
and Amy, with love

First U.S. edition 2008

Library of Congress Cataloging-in-Publication Data is available.

Library of Congress Catalog Card Number 2007038679

ISBN 978-0-7636-3800-9

2 4 6 8 10 9 7 5 3 1

Printed in Singapore

This book was typeset in Veljovic.
The illustrations were done in watercolor and ink.

Candlewick Press
2067 Massachusetts Avenue
Cambridge, Massachusetts 02140

visit us at www.candlewick.com

CANDLEWICK PRESS
CAMBRIDGE, MASSACHUSETTS

MARTHA
IN THE
MIDDLE

Jan Fearnley

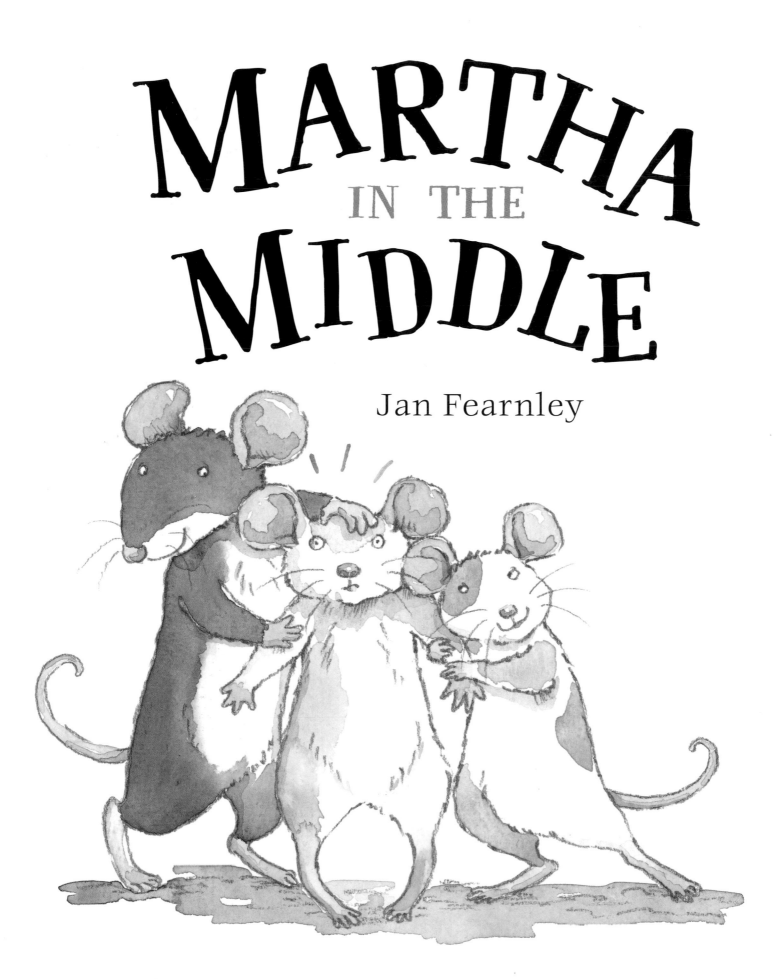

Once there were three little mice.
Clara was the oldest.

Ben was the
youngest.

And then there was Martha.
Martha was in the middle.

In fact, Martha always seemed
to be in the middle of
everything.

When they
played a game,
Martha was in
the middle.

At mealtimes,
Martha sat in the middle.

Sometimes, Martha
was squashed in
the middle,

and even when
Clara and Ben argued,
Martha was in the middle.

Clara was big and sensible.

When she did something good,
everybody said, "What a big, sensible,
grown-up girl."

I'm big and sensible too, thought Martha.

Ben was the baby.

When he did something good,
everybody said, "What a clever,
cutesy-wootsy
little baby."

I'm cutesy-wootsy too,
thought Martha.

When Martha did something good, everybody just said, "Well done, Martha."

Nobody really notices me, thought Martha.

I'm not the biggest. I'm not the baby. I'm just me.

Sometimes she felt invisible.
Sometimes she felt very small.
Sometimes she wanted
to shout,

"Here
I am!"

Squashed in the middle,
stuck in the middle,

she even slept in
the middle.

One day, Martha was really fed up.
She decided to run away to
the far end of the garden.

They won't even care that I'm gone, she thought.

At the end of the garden,
Martha met a frog.

"Hello," said the frog.
"What are you doing here?"

"I've run away," said Martha,
"because I hate being in the
middle! The oldest is
important, and the youngest is
the baby. But the middle
doesn't matter."

The frog tutted.
"I think you're mistaken.
The middle is the
best part."

"Huh?" said Martha.

The frog hopped across the lily pads.
"Let me show you something," he said,
and he dropped a pebble into the pond.

PLOP!

Silver ripples spread from where the pebble had plopped.

"Look where the ripples come from," whispered the frog.

"The middle!" said Martha.

Then they looked at some tall sunflowers. Martha nibbled on some of the sunflower seeds. "See? The seeds are in the middle," said the frog. "That's the best part."

Next, they saw some bees buzzing around some flowers, collecting nectar. Each bee went right to the center of every flower.

"That's the sweetest part," buzzed the bees.

"Right in the middle,"
added the frog.

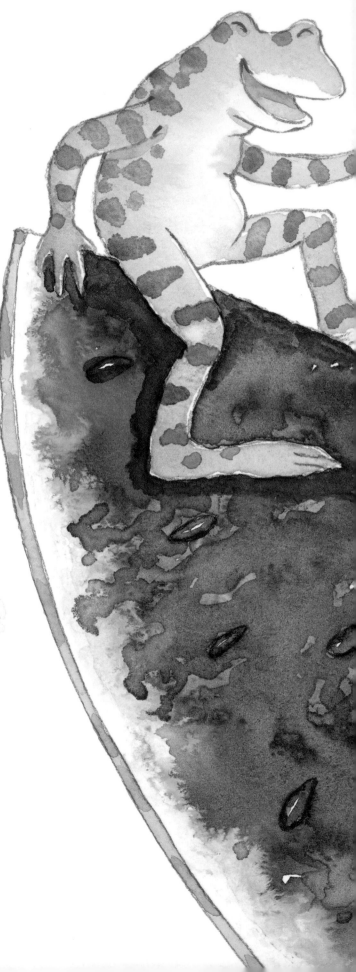

T hey clambered through
the vegetable patch.

"Where are the sweet green
peas hidden?" asked the frog.
"In the middle!" said Martha.

"Where's the juiciest part of
a watermelon?" asked the frog.

"In the middle!"

shouted Martha.

"I think the middle is special," said Martha.

"I think you're right," said the frog, smiling. "And YOU are very special indeed."

Just then, two little faces peered
through the leaves.

"Martha, have you finished running away?" said Clara.

"We miss you," said Ben.

Martha thought for a moment.

"I think I'll run away some
other day," she said to the frog.
"Good-bye!"

It didn't take long before Martha was right back in the middle of things.

And although sometimes she was grown-up and sensible, and sometimes she was cutesy-wootsy . . .

mostly she was happy
being right in the middle . . .

because, as any little frog
will tell you, the middle is
the very **best** place
to be.

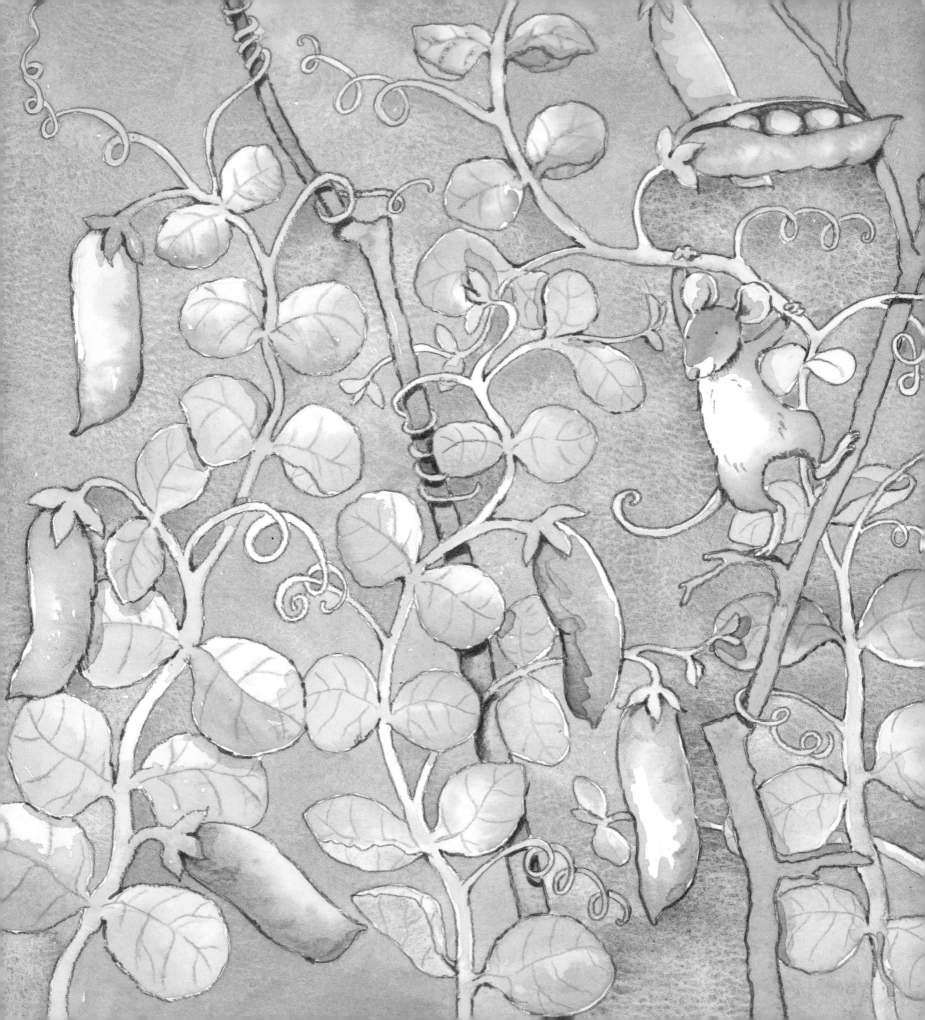